Football is my favourite sport. I've been playing on a team since I was little. I really like being goalie. I'm not the best player, but I have a lot of fun. At least I used to.

This year we're playing with older kids. Most of them are nice. But one player, Francis, can be mean. During matches, Francis gets angry and calls me names if I make a mistake. Football used to be fun, but now it just makes me nervous.

3

We have a match this morning. During warm-ups, I hear a voice near me.
"Hi, Charlie! I mean, four-eyes!"

It's Francis. I pretend I can't hear and run to the pitch.

"Oi, I'm talking to you, fatso," Francis says. **"You'd better not be rubbish today. I want to win!"**

"But ... but it's not all up to me," I say.

"But it's not all up to me," Francis mimics in a high, whiny voice.
"You'd better not ruin our chances – or else!" Francis threatens,
zooming ahead of me.

One way to avoid bullying is to use a
"buddy system". Stick with a friend in
places where bullying occurs. Do the
same for a friend who is being bullied.

Francis' words make it hard to concentrate. I can't even pay attention to what our coach, Mr Thomas is saying. He tells us our positions. I have to ask him to repeat mine.

"Remember what I said, stupid," Francis whispers to me on the pitch. **"No mistakes!"**

I nod, trying to hold back tears. I have to play well today, even if my stomach is in knots.

During the game, my friend Billie passes the ball to me. My heart pounds. It's time to show Francis what I can do. But before I get a chance, a player from the other team wins the ball.

"Charlie, you're so slow!" Francis growls, running after the ball.

The other team scores a goal. **"You're as bad as Charlie!"** I hear Franics yell at the goalie.

Francis' words ring in my ears. Maybe I *am* really rubbish. Maybe I shouldn't play football any more.

Name-calling and insults are very hurtful. People who are bullied sometimes start to believe what they hear, even if it isn't true.

It's my turn to be in goal. Five minutes from the end of the match, the score is one all. I'm so nervous, I feel like throwing up.

Francis and Billie keep the ball at the other team's end. But they can't score. Now there are only two minutes left.

Uh oh. The other team has won the ball. They're heading my way. The players weave in and out. I lose track of the ball until it sails past my head into the net behind me. The whistle blows. The other team wins the match.

It's bad enough that we lost the match. But I know Francis will blame me.

"**Nice job, idiot!**" Francis shouts sarcastically after the others have left. "**Charlie, you're so slow! You're not a rabbit. You're a tortoise!**"

I feel terrible. I start to cry. It makes things worse.

"**Crying won't help, baby,**" Francis says. "**Wah, wah!**" Francis mocks me and walks away.

Everyone thinks I'm crying because of the result. But we've lost matches before. It's just that no one has made me feel bad about losing before.

It can be hard not to cry or show fear when being bullied. But the person who is bullying wants you to feel upset and afraid. If you can pretend you're not upset or ignore the bully, he or she might give up.

Mr Thomas tells us we played a really good team.
The rest of my teammates aren't mean to me, but I can
tell they're disappointed.

"It's not your fault, Charlie. We all lost the match," says Billie.

"Francis blames me," I sniff.

"Francis is being a bully," Billie says. "I think you should talk to Mr Thomas about it."

I shake my head no. **"That will just make things worse,"** I say. **"I think I should just give up football."**

"But you love football!" Billie says. **"We have so much fun playing."**

"Not any more," I say.

If you or someone else is being bullied, it's always best to tell an adult you trust. The adult can stop the bullying behaviour and get everyone the help they need.

On Monday I'm afraid to face Francis at football practice. I call my dad and tell him I feel sick. He picks me up so that I don't have to go.

On Wednesday Mr Thomas finds me in the corridor after school.

"Charlie, Billie told me that you're thinking about giving up football," Mr Thomas says. I nod. "Billie also said it's because Francis is being mean to you," he says.

I nod again. Then I start to cry.

"I'm very sorry you've been bullied, Charlie," Mr Thomas says. "Sport should be fun, and teammates should support each other. I promise to put an end to this, OK?"

Before football practice, Mr Thomas sits the team down. He explains that calling people names, saying mean things and threatening people are examples of bullying. Mr Thomas tells us how to be good teammates. He also says that anyone caught bullying another player will miss the next match.

Billie winks at me. I smile back.
I hope this works.

Mr Thomas thinks I should tell my parents about being bullied. He says he will help me.

"Verbal bullying can be just as hurtful as physical bullying," says Mr Thomas during the meeting with my parents.

I nod. I know how horrible it feels. Mr Thomas says that I might feel sad for a while. If I do, I should talk to him or my parents.

"And tell one of us if this happens again. OK, Charlie?" Mr Thomas says.

People who have been bullied often feel sad or bad about themselves. This can last a long time. Some people need help to get over these feelings. If you've been bullied, talk to a parent or teacher about how you feel.

Francis was left out of the team today because of bullying. I was worried that everyone would think I was a coward. But no one said anything, including Francis.

"You were right about telling Mr Thomas, Billie," I say after the match. **"Thanks for doing that."**

"That's what friends are for," says Billie. **"Well played today!"**

It's nice to have so many people on my side. I'm feeling better already. I think playing football will be fun again soon.